KOBA
GHOUL OF THE SHADOWS

BY ADAM BLADE

ICY
MOUNTAIN
REGION
ERRINEL

The Warrior's Road
COSHTIN PROVINCE
PYRUS
HE
LAST
CITY
MARBLE CASTLE

Greetings, whoever reads this.

I am Tanner, Avantia's first Master of the Beasts. I fear I have little time left. My life slips away, and I write these few words as a testament for whoever may come across my remains. I have reached the end of my final journey. But a new warrior's journey is just beginning...

With the death of a Master, a new hero must take on the responsibility of guarding the kingdom of Avantia. Avantia needs a true warrior to wear the Golden Armour. He or she must walk the Warrior's Road – a test of valour and strength. I have succeeded, but it has cost me my life. I only hope those who follow survive.

May fortune be with you,

Tanner

PROLOGUE

Sixty years ago...

The gateway of the castle opened like a gaping mouth, and a wide path of glowing cobblestones ran from it like a glimmering red tongue.

The young wizard in the green robe turned, his eyes following the track through the rugged landscape of rocks and ravines.

"Why should I, Jezrin, travel the long hard path of the Warrior's Road?"

he said, with a sneer. "Magic is *so* much quicker!"

A cry of pain sounded from the other side of the open gate. *I'm just in time,* he thought, as he ran through the gate into a wide courtyard. On the cobbles, a man in golden armour lay groaning in agony. Jezrin crouched beside him, running his fingers over the gold.

"A suit of magical armour would be most useful to me," he said, prising open the visor on the helmet. He gazed pitilessly down at the man's face. The eyes were dim, but breath was still rasping between gritted teeth.

"Not quite dead yet, eh?" said Jezrin. "But very close, I think." He smiled. "You won't need this finery any more." He began to tug the golden gauntlets off the man's hands.

A great roar filled the courtyard, shaking the ground and echoing loudly between the walls. Jezrin's stomach knotted with fear.

He glanced up in time to see a mighty fist swinging through the air.

Yelping with terror, Jezrin flung himself across the dying knight's chest. He felt the wind of the sweeping arm on his neck.

A moment slower and my head would have been torn from my shoulders!

He scrambled to his feet, staring up at a terrible form that towered over him.

It was a great Beast. From beneath heavy curved brows, two eyes stared down at him. One eye glowed as green as poison, the other blazed orange like fire. Jezrin's chest tightened with dread.

"Koba, Ghoul of the Shadows!" he gasped.

The Beast's mouth twisted into a grimace, the stench of his breath almost knocking Jezrin from his feet. Koba's massive leathery head was crowned with spikes and one of his huge pointed ears was hung with golden rings. Muscular arms reached down, the snatching fingers tipped with double claws like the tails of scorpions.

Jezrin grabbed the dying knight's hand, and tried to drag him away across the courtyard. *I've not come all this way to flee empty-handed,* he thought. *I will have the power of the Master of the Beasts, if it's the last thing I do!*

Koba's orange and green eyes pulsed with evil delight. Jezrin had only taken a few paces when a mind-shredding pain flared behind his eyes.

"Arrgh!"

Releasing the knight's hand, Jezrin

dropped to his knees, clutching his head. A voice burned deep in his skull:

"You have not walked the Warrior's Road. You do not deserve to be here."

Jezrin felt his body leave the ground. He opened his eyes and found that he was hanging upside down from his ankles, suspended from Koba's forked fingertips.

He heard a distant cracking sound and saw the sky being torn open. Through the ragged hole, he glimpsed the palace of King Theo of Avantia.

"No!" he cried. "I'm not ready to go back!"

With a flick of his powerful wrist, the Beast flung Jezrin towards the sky-portal.

The Wizard managed to twist around in midair.

"Beware, Koba!" he shouted. "You have not seen the last of me! I shall return – and Avantia *will* be mine!"

CHAPTER ONE

THE DESERTED CASTLE

The Hooded Man's words rang in Tom's mind as he stared across the ruins of the Last City.

The Road is a trick. It never ends.

Tom turned and saw his own doubt mirrored in Elenna's face. Silver lay with his muzzle between his paws, his sad eyes turned up towards them.

"Well?" asked the Hooded Man.

"What is your decision?"

Biting his lip, Tom looked into the man's blue eyes.

They're just like my *eyes...*

Tom was still reeling. The Hooded Man had followed them down the Road, but he'd only just revealed his true identity. The Hooded Man was Tom's future self, beaten and weighed down by many years of walking the Warrior's Road.

It can't be real, Tom thought. *Is this how I'll look one day?*

But despite the ancient scars and the broken nose, Tom had to admit – this man looked so much like him.

There was a sudden cracking sound and Tom turned sharply. A dark hole, outlined with silver light, had appeared under the pillars of a collapsed arch.

The next portal, Tom thought. On each

stage of this Quest, Tom had had to step through a magical doorway.

"You'll press on, despite my warning?" sneered the Hooded Man. "Then you truly are the greatest fool ever to walk this Road!"

"Maybe I am," Tom said. "But I never turn away from a Quest."

And if I don't prove myself worthy of being the Master of the Beasts, the Judge will conquer Avantia.

He caught Elenna by the hand. "Follow me," he whispered. Then he seized the Hooded Man's wrist.

"What new stupidity is this?" cried the old warrior.

The dark portal loomed over them. "You're coming with us," said Tom. "Two Toms are better than one!" Then he gave a hard yank, pulling the two of them with him.

"No!" The older man tried to drag himself back, but Tom plunged through the archway.

He shut his eyes against a sudden blinding light. When he opened them again, he found himself squinting up at a high wall of smooth black marble. It was a castle, with great towers and battlements and turrets. Glowing red cobbles led to a massive gatehouse.

The Warrior's Road.

Tom released his grip on Elenna, and on the Hooded Man. He marched in through the gate, keeping a grip on the hilt of his sword. Elenna and Silver were at his side. He glanced over his shoulder to make sure that his future self was still following. *This is like nothing I've ever encountered before!* he thought.

Inside was a courtyard, with more

black walls rising on every side. At the far side of the courtyard, a trestle table was laid with steaming pies and fresh loaves of bread. There were platters of fried fish, and overflowing bowls of fresh vegetables.

"It's as though everyone just

vanished in the middle of a normal day," said Elenna. She pointed. "There's even a filled dog bowl on the ground."

"Hello?" Tom shouted.

His voice echoed around the courtyard, but no one came in response to his call. Silence fell, as though the castle were holding its breath.

Waiting to pounce...

Silver bounded over to the bowl and ate hungrily.

"Silver, careful," called Elenna. "It might be bad."

"He would know tainted food by its smell," said Tom, sniffing the aromas that drifted from the table. "I think this is all good to eat."

The Hooded Man shoved past Tom and strode to the table. He picked up a large pie in both hands and took a bite.

"Apple pie!" he mumbled through a mouthful. "It's good! Just like Aunt Maria used to bake!"

Elenna gave Tom a puzzled glance. He knew exactly what she was thinking, because he was thinking the same thing:

Aunt Maria's speciality is cherry *pie.*

Frowning, Elenna walked up to the older Tom, looking him up and down.

"What are you goggling at?" he sneered, before taking another bite.

"A greedy man," said Elenna. She looked towards Tom, nodding at the Hooded Man's sword.

Tom understood in a moment.

His sword is on his right *hip – I wear mine on my left.*

He began to look more carefully at the man. Where his collar hung open,

Tom saw a long, deep scar that ran from his throat to his shoulder.

"How did you get that scar?" asked Tom.

"It was in a battle with a Beast," the Hooded Man muttered, not meeting Tom's eyes. "A Beast called...erm, Arctune. A fearsome monster that dwelled in the land of…of…Gwiltia…to the far south of Avantia."

"I've never heard of Gwiltia," said Tom.

"How could you? It hasn't happened to you yet," said the man impatiently.

"But I've seen maps of Avantia and all the realms that surround it – and there is no land called Gwiltia."

"He's right!" said Elenna, taking her bow off her shoulder and setting an arrow to the string. "Besides – how could you have visited a land to the far south of Avantia if you never left the Warrior's Road?"

The Hooded Man stared at her in silence.

Tom drew his sword. "Tell us the truth," he demanded.

The man's cloak started to twitch and writhe. Deep in the shadows of the hood, his eyes glowed and grew, changing colour.

Tom gave a gasp as he saw one green eye and one orange eye glaring at him.

Silver growled and bared his teeth.

"Stay back!" Tom shouted. "He's transforming!"

A moment later the dark cloak exploded into a seething mass of snakes. Hissing and spitting, the snakes slithered away while the Hooded Man's form began to bulge, ripping through his clothing to reveal the

leathery skin beneath.

His head swelled too, his ears growing pointed, and hung with golden rings. His legs seemed to vanish, wreathed in swirling smoke.

The mouth stretched into a hideous expression that was half fury and half mocking smile. Tom stumbled back

from a blast of reeking breath. The Beast's arms unfolded and the fingers flexed to reveal long forked claws.

A fearsome voice burst into Tom's head.

"My name is Koba, and you have proved yourself a worthy opponent!"

CHAPTER TWO

THE DEADLY MAZE

It was all a trick – a disguise!

The Hooded Man was not Tom's future self. He had been a Beast all along.

Before Tom was able to draw his blade, Koba's huge fist struck him in the stomach.

Tom let out a gasp of pain as he slid backwards across the courtyard, doubled up and fighting for breath. He crashed against a wall, his stomach knotted in agony.

He heard Silver snarling angrily, as a loosed arrow whooshed through the air. His friends were fighting back.

Tom staggered to his feet. Koba glided across the courtyard. His huge upper body was solid and muscular, but his lower half was wreathed in a whirlwind of amber smoke. Silver bounded after him as Elenna let loose another arrow. It glided over Koba's shoulder and the tip chinked off one of the marble walls. Silver strayed close to the whirling smoke and was thrown, tumbling, across the flagstones.

"Keep back!" Tom shouted to his friends. "Let me face the Beast."

With a roar, half laughter and half rage, Koba vanished through the doorway of a round tower in the corner of the courtyard.

Ignoring the pain in his stomach, Tom raced after him. The doorway led to a stone staircase that spiralled up into deep gloom. Tom pounded up the stairs, soon finding himself surrounded by utter blackness. He could hardly see the steps beneath his feet.

He climbed slowly, listening for any sound of the Beast. Elenna's feet pattered behind him.

Tom lifted a foot for the next step, but with a cry he felt the weight of his body plunge into emptiness. He toppled forward, just managing to snatch hold of the final step with one hand.

Daylight flooded into the tower, and Tom gasped in horror. He was hanging by his fingertips over a deadly drop.

Koba had led him into a trap.

The stairway leads nowhere!

Tom gritted his teeth as the strength seeped from his grip.

Elenna's face appeared above him. "Hold on!" she said, reaching to grab his arm and drag him up. No sooner had she heaved him to safety than the step collapsed and plunged into the blackness below.

Then the step they were resting on began to crumble, too.

"The whole staircase is collapsing!" Tom shouted. "We have to get out of here!"

They raced down the stairway, step after step crashing into dust behind them as they ran.

Tom saw a small doorway in the tower's wall. Catching hold of Elenna, he flung himself through. Silver leaped after them just as the rest of the stairway fell from under his paws.

Tom gazed around himself. They had entered a long hall with soaring marble walls and tall, arched windows.

But something is wrong about this place.

There were windows set into the

floor, and doors placed high on the walls where they couldn't be reached. Sets of steps led up to blank stone walls and other stairways hung upside down from the vaulted ceiling. Tom's mind reeled, trying to take it all in.

"This Beast must be a shape-shifter," he said, edging forward. "First of all, he tried to make me turn back by pretending to be my future self. When that didn't work, he brought us here to lure me to my death."

Tom had hardly finished speaking when Silver let out a snarl and scampered towards a doorway in the far wall.

"He must have smelled something," Elenna said, running after the wolf.

"Wait!" called Tom. "This whole castle is some kind of magical maze –

you can't trust anything you see!"

But Elenna had vanished through the doorway.

Tom followed anxiously, stepping into a long corridor – but there was no sign of Elenna or Silver.

How is that possible? She was right here...

He ran on, coming to a point where five new corridors led off in different directions.

"Elenna!" he shouted. "Silver!"

He turned and found the way back blocked by a stone wall. His corridor had vanished.

Then he saw Elenna running towards him.

"Thank goodness I found you!" Tom gasped.

Then he saw movement from the corner of his eye. He turned. Another

Elenna was racing towards him along a second corridor with relief in her eyes, and Silver by her side.

"Tom! I thought I'd never find you," she cried. Her mouth dropped open in horror as she pointed over his shoulder. "Look out!"

Tom spun around to see that the first Elenna was aiming an arrow at him. She loosed the bowstring. Tom brought up his shield to protect himself and the arrow thudded into the wood.

Then the first Elenna's skin began to swell and turn yellow.

"Koba!" Tom gasped as the Beast's leathery, muscular form returned, his smoky lower body filling the corridor.

Silver leaped with a snarl, but Koba spun around, his arm missing the wolf by a fraction as his claws raked

at the marble wall.

"Are you going to stand and fight this time?" Tom shouted at the Beast.

Koba's wide mouth opened and a bellow of laughter shook the corridor.

The stones beneath the Beast cracked then fell away. Koba dropped into the hole. Tom flung himself forward, but the stones rose back into position, the cracks sealing over. He fell down on his knees, beating at the stones with his sword and shield, desperate to break through.

Elenna tried to help him prise the stones apart while Silver scrabbled with his claws.

"It's hopeless," Tom said. "How can I fight a Beast who can look like anyone he chooses, and who can escape through solid walls?" He stood up, tingling with frustration. "Koba! Come and do battle with me!"

The castle was silent.

Tom looked around and realised that their surroundings had changed again. They were at the hub of a dozen or more corridors, leading away like the spokes of a wheel.

"Which way should we go now?" asked Elenna.

Tom turned in a slow circle. A red

glow caught his eye, running across the end of one of the corridors.

The Warrior's Road.

"That way!" he said, racing towards the red light. "If we follow the Road, the Beast will *have* to come to us." As he set foot on the glowing red pathway, he heard Silver growl behind him.

Elenna's voice trembled as she said, "I think he already has!"

CHAPTER THREE

THE SHAPE-SHIFTER'S VICTORY

Tom spun around. Koba towered over them, his arms folded, his mismatched eyes gleaming with evil amusement.

Tom leaped in front of Elenna, raising his shield and aiming his sword at the Beast's broad chest. The whirlwind of amber smoke beneath Koba flicked from side to side where it touched the floor, lashing like an angry tail.

Koba glided away from Tom's slashing blade with a fiendish grin. The Beast raised his arm and drove his fist into the arched roof. Splinters of marble rained down.

Tom felt a searing pain in his cheek. He heard Elenna cry out and saw her stumble onto one knee, clutching her arm. Silver howled in panic.

"Are you all right?" Tom shouted, as warm blood trickled down his face.

"Yes," gasped Elenna. "Just a scratch."

Tom lofted his sword, but Koba's arm swept down, knocking the blade aside while his other hand reached out with its forked claws.

Strong fingers closed around Tom's chest, hoisting him into the air and squeezing the breath out of him. As

Koba laughed, foul breath blasted over Tom's face.

The Beast lunged forward with his other hand to catch hold of Elenna, snapping her bow in two as he snatched her up.

Koba swept them both towards his ugly, misshapen face. Elenna struggled, beating at the hand that gripped her and kicking helplessly at the air.

Koba shook her hard and Elenna yelped then fell still, her head lolling and her face twisted in pain.

The Beast laughed and thick spittle splashed on Tom's face. Koba brought his hands closer to his face, his mouth opening and his fangs dripping saliva.

Koba's voice echoed in Tom's mind.

"I have slaughtered more warriors than you could ever imagine. I shall bite off your heads, chew them up and spit them out!"

Tom recoiled in horror as the Beast thrust him into his stinking mouth.

But the teeth did not bite down. Instead, Koba let out a roar of pain that rattled Tom's eardrums. The Beast's fingers loosened just enough for Tom to lift his sword and stab at them,

sliding out of Koba's grasp as thick amber blood oozed from the wounds.

Tom swung himself towards Elenna's dangling legs, catching hold of them and pulling her free of Koba's grip. They crashed to the floor, gasping for breath. Now Tom saw the reason for the Beast's bellow of agony.

Silver had sunk his teeth into Koba's upper arm. The wolf was hanging in the air, his paws kicking and his jaws clamped tight on the Beast's flesh while globs of amber blood trickled down.

The Beast flung himself from side to side as he glided away along the corridor. Then he tossed Silver loose. The wolf landed neatly on his paws and raced back towards them.

Koba was grunting and snarling in confusion and pain, his shoulders hunched, his mismatched eyes glaring furiously at his foes.

"I'll finish this right now," Tom said. He strode towards the Beast, but his steps faltered as Koba's shape began to writhe and dwindle.

Tom staggered back as a new form faced him. A human form, tall and bearded – a man he knew all too well.

"Father!" Tom gasped, his heart pounding in his chest as he gazed at his own father. "But...it can't be..."

The last time Tom had seen his father, Taladon had been sprawled on a frozen plain, his life's blood staining the ice around him.

"You were *always* a disappointment to me," said Taladon.

Tom's soul shrivelled at the sound of his father's voice.

No! This is another one of Koba's tricks.

All the same, he couldn't bring

himself to fight the vision before him.

"I wanted my son to make me proud," Taladon continued, pointing a finger at Tom. "But when it mattered, you let me die."

Guilt wrenched at Tom's heart. He let his sword arm fall and his blade hang at his side. *He's right. I did fail him.*

"Tom, this is not real!" cried Elenna. "You mustn't believe him." She was shaking with anger. "What kind of twisted monster are you?" she shouted at the Beast who wore Taladon's form.

Koba's horrible laughter sounded from Taladon's mouth.

"My son knows he is responsible for my death," he said. "As his spirit weakens, so mine grows stronger." He laughed again. "Tom, my boy – you know I speak the truth. Your Beast Quest is over..."

CHAPTER FOUR

THE ROOM OF COFFINS

"No!" Tom shouted, fighting his despair. "It may be true that I couldn't save my father, but he would *never* tell me to give up on a Quest!" He glared at the vision of Taladon. "You are *not* my father."

As Tom ran at his enemy, he saw Taladon's eyes gleam orange and green as he stepped backwards with a snarl.

His body began to shrink and change once more.

Tom raised his sword, ready to strike. But when he saw at the last moment, he pulled away, unable to set his sword in the flesh of the old man who now stood gazing sadly at him.

"Aduro!" Tom groaned, staring in disbelief at the ancient form of the former Wizard who had been his friend and mentor. "No." He shook his head. "This isn't real."

Aduro's red-rimmed eyes welled with tears as he gazed at Tom. "It's your fault my magic was taken away from me."

Tom staggered, trembling in shock.

This isn't real. That's not Aduro.

But although his mind knew the truth, his heart could not bring himself to fight the man who had given him his very first Beast Quest.

"I was wrong to think you could become a hero," Aduro said. "The kingdoms need a true champion – instead, they got a halfwit blacksmith's apprentice."

Anger boiled through Tom's veins, but he could not manage to attack the opponent in front of him. The appearance of Aduro was too perfect. Too convincing.

"Remember why you're here, Tom!" he heard Elenna call from behind him. "You're earning the title of Master of the Beasts!'

The forms of dozens of Beasts flashed through Tom's mind; the countless battles he had fought. *Every battle ended in my victory,* he told himself, looking back to the vision of Aduro. Orange and green lights glowed deep within his narrowed eyes.

The more I believe in myself, Tom realised, *the harder it is for Koba to keep up his deception.*

He launched himself at Aduro, knocked the old man off his feet and sent them both sprawling to the floor.

Tom knelt astride the narrow chest, pressing down with his shield as the former Wizard struggled beneath.

"If you take an old man's form, you can only have an old man's strength!" Tom cried, lifting his sword. "Yield to me, Koba!"

The shrivelled shape began to swell up under him. In a few moments the chest was too broad for Tom to straddle. He teetered, losing his balance as Koba surged upwards with a roar of anger.

One huge hand swiped Tom's sword from his grasp, sending it skittering across the floor. The other hand snatched at Tom while the mouth opened in a stinking hiss.

But Tom wasn't about to let himself be caught a second time. He ducked under the groping fingers and somersaulted off the Beast's chest.

Tom landed neatly on the ground, but his momentum took him stumbling away from his sword. Koba rose to his full height, his head almost touching the ceiling and his arms reaching out.

Elenna appeared behind the Beast with Silver, and picked up Tom's sword.

Tom took a deep breath, bracing himself as Koba glided forward on his whirl of cloud. His clawed fingers were flexed.

At the last possible moment, Tom darted sideways, bouncing off the wall and using Koba's shoulder to vault high over the Beast and to the other side.

Koba wheeled around, bellowing in fury.

"Where to?" panted Elenna, reaching

out to hand Tom his sword.

A passage to his left caught Tom's eye. It seemed to be made entirely of crystal. With the Beast bearing down, there was nowhere else to go.

"This way," he said, racing down the glinting corridor.

They came to a tall arched door of pure, clear glass. They passed through and Tom closed the door behind them. A glass key was in the lock. When Tom turned it, he heard a sound like a chime.

"It won't keep Koba at bay for long," he said.

The room took his breath away. Rows of glass coffins floated in the chill air.

Elenna had fallen silent and Silver was pressed against her, his head down and his tail between his legs.

"There's death in this place," murmured Tom.

He began to walk down the aisle between the coffins. Each contained the body of a man in armour.

"They've been dead a long time," Tom said, gazing at the white face of a man wrapped in a pale blue shroud. "But

they're perfectly preserved – as though they died yesterday."

"It reminds me of the Gallery of Tombs," said Elenna.

Tom nodded. "I think I know what this place is," he said. "This is where all the warriors who died on the Road are laid to rest."

They came to the end of the long, solemn rows of coffins. The final one stood open and empty.

Tom blood froze when he saw words inscribed on the glass lid: *Tom of Errinel.*

CHAPTER FIVE

WARRIOR IN CHAINS

My own coffin, waiting for me.

Tom stepped forward and slammed down the coffin lid. A hollow ringing sound filled the chamber and chill air wafted around them.

"I will never lie here among these corpses!" he said, raising his sword to smash the coffin that bore his name.

He became still when he heard a

strange noise. He looked at Elenna. "What was that?"

"It sounded like someone groaning," she replied.

Silver darted off, scurrying beneath the coffins towards a small frosted-glass door in the side wall of the chamber. The two of them ran after the wolf, who was now scrabbling at the bottom of the door. Elenna reached for the glass handle.

"Be careful," Tom warned her. "Trust nothing."

The door swung open into a small chamber of rough, silvery crystal.

A man was sprawled against the far wall, his head lolling on his chest and long straggly hair dangling over his face. His arms were raised, and Tom saw that they were chained to the wall by crystal manacles.

"Is he dead?" Elenna whispered.

Silver slunk towards the man, his muzzle low. He sniffed the raised hands cautiously, and stumbled back warily when the man's fingers twitched.

This could be another of Koba's tricks, Tom thought, walking slowly towards the man. "Who are you?" he asked.

The man lifted his head, and dark eyes gazed up through matted hair. His lips moved as though he was trying to speak. His black gaze was full of fear.

Surely he can't be dangerous?

"Don't move," said Tom, lifting his sword and turning to Elenna. "Hold that manacle so I can smash it open."

Elenna stepped forward and angled one of the crystal manacles so that Tom could strike it without injuring the prisoner. He brought his sword-hilt down sharply. The crystal rang and sparked, but did not break.

The man spoke, his voice weak and rasping. "You mustn't try to free me."

"I can't leave you at Koba's mercy," said Tom.

The man gave a weary smile. "Trust me, Koba is no threat to me," he said, his voice gaining in strength. "I defeated him almost four centuries ago."

Tom stared down at the man. "You defeated him?" he said in amazement. But the Judge had told them only a handful of people had ever completed the Warrior's Road. "Then are you..."

"Tanner," said the man. He coughed, the breath rattling in his throat. "I am he. Or I was, once."

Tom let out a gasp. *The first Master of the Beasts!*

"How can you be?" asked Elenna, staring at the man. "Tanner is dead. His body lies in the Gallery of Tombs."

"As you can see, I am not dead,"

said the man. "The tale of my death was created to protect my reputation."

"I don't understand," said Tom.

"Defeating Koba took everything I had – body *and* soul," said the man, pulling himself up so that he was sitting with his back to the wall. "But after I vanquished him, something in me had changed. It happened slowly – a flare of temper, the red mist of anger filling my mind... The desire to kill Beasts rather than simply tame them." His eyes darkened. "The lust for carnage!"

"The battle with Koba did something bad to you," said Tom.

"Yes," agreed Tanner. "And, when I felt Evil overwhelm me, I returned to this place – to Koba's lair – and locked myself in this room so that

I would be able to do no more harm to anyone – man or Beast." He hung his head in shame, then raised it to look at Tom. "And so that I could warn others who travel the Warrior's Road."

"Warn them of what?" Tom asked.

"To turn back from this Quest," said Tanner. "Koba is no ordinary Beast," he went on. "He cannot be beaten – because even those who defeat him eventually succumb to Evil!"

Tom was stunned by what he was hearing.

Tanner is said to be the greatest warrior Avantia has ever known. If even he *fell prey to Koba's terrible powers, then what chance do I have?*

"The Judge meant for you to turn Evil," Elenna murmured, staring at Tom. "That's why he ended the ban on anyone walking the Warrior's Road."

Tom took deep breaths to calm the rage rising in his chest. "But I have to fight the Beast," he said, "whatever the outcome. If I don't, Avantia will have no Master of the Beasts – and Evil will rule the kingdom." He strode towards the door of the cell. "I cannot fail." He stopped in the doorway. "Elenna – you and Silver must stay with Tanner. I have to walk the rest of the Warrior's Road alone."

"Do not face this Beast!" called Tanner.

"I must," said Tom, turning back towards the chamber of glass coffins.

"Then heed my words," called Tanner. "You may succeed in defeating Koba, but your victory will come at a terrible price."

Tom did not turn around. "And what price is that?" he asked.

"Your very soul," said Tanner.

CHAPTER SIX

A PAINFUL DECEPTION

Tom strode between the glass coffins and unlocked the door. The castle was silent again.

"You're a coward, Koba!" Tom shouted into the long corridor. "Whose shape will you hide behind next?"

A fearsome roar burst out behind him. Koba crashed down through the glass ceiling of the coffin room. Tom

threw his shield up over his face as the Beast swept around the room on his whirlwind of cloud, smashing the coffins and scattering the bodies of the dead heroes. Tom looked in horror and outrage at the corpses strewn across the chamber floor.

"No!" he shouted, raising his sword.

"I won't let you do this."

He sprang forward, glass crunching under his feet.

When he was still ten paces away, Koba began to shrink into the form of a tall, cloaked figure. A beautiful face, framed with long dark hair, looked at Tom with kind eyes. He stopped short.

"Mother!"

"Yes, Tom," said the familiar soft and gentle voice. Freya drew back the folds of her cloak to reveal shining silver armour. "I have come to apologise for not being there for you when you were growing up." She gave a sad smile. "Can you ever forgive me?"

"This is a trick!" Tom shouted, his whole body shaking with anger.

Freya moved slowly towards him, still smiling warmly. "I know how my absence hurt you," she sighed. "You thought you were an orphan for so many years."

A pang of hurt stabbed Tom's heart, as sharp as the splintered glass that surrounded him. He set his jaw, fighting the emotions that threatened to overwhelm him.

My mother had important duties to

perform, he reminded himself. *It was not her fault that she wasn't there.*

"I was always proud of you, and never more so than today," she said. "You have proved your bravery, Tom. Go home, my son. Do not risk your soul on this foolish Quest."

"No." Tom averted his eyes as she came closer. "This is just an illusion."

"Trust in me," said Freya. "I will lead you home to Avantia. We will defeat the Judge together, and restore goodness and joy to the kingdom." Her smile widened. "That's what your father would have wanted."

Tom stared at the perfect image. He wanted so much to believe it was real. She was only a couple of paces away now, the broken glass tinkling with every step she took. But just behind her, a larger shard of glass was embedded upright in the floor – and in the dim reflection it cast, Tom saw that she held two knives behind her back.

"No!" He bounded backwards as her arms swept around, the daggers slicing towards his chest.

How could I have fallen for the Beast's tricks again?

Her face now a mask of fury, Freya flung herself forward, her eyes

glowing orange and green, her lips drawn back from her teeth. "Come to my arms, my son!" she raved, spittle flecking her chin. "Let me show you just how much I love you!"

Tom sprang aside, sweeping the two daggers away with his sword. But his opponent was as quick as a snake. She ducked under his shield, aiming one dagger up under his ribs while the other slashed at his throat.

He twisted away from one, and took the other on his shield. But he couldn't bring himself to stab at Freya. She lunged again, the blades glittering as they scythed towards his face.

Tom thrust his shield up, his arms jarring at the impact of the blades. One knife edged past his shield and nicked his neck. He hissed with pain and scrambled back, horrified by the malice in his mother's eyes. She gnashed her teeth and charged at him like a wild animal.

As she attacked, he thrust his shield into her stomach, sending her skidding across the glass-strewn floor. He bounded after her and aimed his sword at her heart.

"Tom, my son, don't hurt me!" she pleaded.

"I won't," he said, "but you must yield."

She writhed on the floor, swinging her legs around and sweeping his feet out from under him. As he fell, she was on him in an instant, aiming both knives at his face.

Tom kicked her off and sent her crashing into a pile of broken coffins. He got to his feet again as a fearful howl tore through the air.

Silver!

Tom spun around, and ran for the crystal cell.

Inside, he found the wolf crouching beside Elenna. His friend was slumped on the ground, blood flowing from a cut above her eye. The manacles hung open on the wall.

"Tanner broke free," Elenna mumbled in a daze. "He attacked me and ran."

The evil in him must have grown stronger, thought Tom.

He stood up, despair weighing heavy in his heart.

"So now I have two enemies," he said. "The most dangerous Beast of them all – and Avantia's greatest ever warrior."

This would truly be the deadliest battle of his life.

CHAPTER SEVEN

TWO TERRIBLE ENEMIES

Elenna struggled to her feet, wiping the blood from her forehead.

"You should stay and rest," said Tom.

She shook her head. "Nothing is going to keep me out of this fight."

Tom smiled, a little of the weight of this Quest lifting from his shoulders. "Then keep close to me," he said.

"I need a new weapon," said Elenna.

"My bow is broken."

Silver pawed a crystal manacle on its long chain, looking up at her. Tom used his sword to hack the chain from the wall. Elenna swung it around her head like a deadly, weighted whip.

"This will do fine," she said.

There was no sign of Freya or the Beast in the ruins of the coffin chamber. Tom headed through the broken door, Elenna at his side and Silver prowling watchfully after.

They walked the corridors of the castle, and Tom recognised nothing that he saw. "Everything has changed again since we came here," he said. "For all we know, the castle could be leading us around in circles."

"Or guiding us into a trap," muttered Elenna.

Tom paused when he heard the faint clash of metal on metal. He closed his eyes to pinpoint the direction from which the sounds were coming.

"This way," he said, running up a flight of steps and through a series of empty rooms, hearing Elenna and Silver close behind.

They emerged onto a balcony high above a great hall. In the grand chamber below, Tanner and Koba were engaged in battle. Tanner was lunging and stabbing with his sword while Koba darted across the floor on his whirling cloud of smoke, warding the blows off with his arms and snatching at Tanner with his claws.

"I'm going to kill you this time, Koba!" Tanner shouted, his face a mask of battle fury.

Tom leaned over the balcony, his heart racing.

"This is *my* Quest," he said. "I cannot let Tanner kill Koba."

There was a curving stairway at either end of the long balcony. Tom raced to the closest stairway and ran down it.

But as he neared the foot of the stairs, they twisted and whirled beneath him.

Tom stumbled back up to the balcony.

"Koba knows we're here," said Elenna. "He's changing the castle to stop us from getting down there."

Tom heard Koba's voice in his head again, projected there by the red jewel.

"I will have revenge... Tanner must die!"

"Koba's changing!" cried Elenna.

Tom stared as the Beast shrivelled down to the form of a stooped, white-haired old lady clad in a shabby cloak.

Tanner fell back, his sword shaking in his hands. "Grandmother?" he gasped.

"I read about Tanner's grandmother, Esme, in the *Chronicles of Avantia*," said Elenna. "She died trying to protect him from Evil forces."

"My sweet grandson!" cried the old lady. "Come to me!"

"No!" Tanner howled. "You won't fool me again, Koba! No matter what form you take, I will slay you!" He swung his sword at the old lady's neck.

Esme bounded back, drawing out a huge axe from under the folds of her cloak. The chamber walls shook as axe met sword with a ringing clash. Tanner swung again. The old lady darted to the side, bringing her axe up

to deflect the blade. Sparks flew as she cackled with laughter and twisted on her heels.

"We have to get to them before they kill each other!" cried Elenna.

"I have an idea," said Tom. He pointed to the stairway on the right of the balcony. "You and Silver go that way, and I'll take the other stairs… We might be able to confuse Koba."

Elenna and Silver ran for one set of stairs, while Tom leaped down the other. He was halfway down when he felt the room shifting.

Not this time!

He flexed his legs and sprang sideways off the stairs, leaping across to Elenna and Silver's staircase. He hopped down the remaining steps and ran towards the two combatants.

Tanner was twice the size of Esme,

but the old lady was lithe and serpent-quick. She swung the axe at his feet so Tanner had to leap high, then darted aside as his sword came down, ringing on the marble floor.

"We'll take Tanner," said Elenna. "You deal with the Beast!"

Esme swung the axe at neck height, forcing Tanner back. Elenna dived in close, twirling the chain around her head then flinging it across the floor.

The chain coiled around Tanner's ankles and snapped tight. He stumbled and fell with a cry. Tom leaped over him, sword and shield ready.

The old lady drew back, her mouth widening in a horrible grin. As Tom watched, the mouth expanded, twisting the face hideously before the whole shape of the old lady burst apart and Koba was once more looming

above him, shrieking with laughter on a pillar of swirling smoke.

The Beast still had the axe in his hands, but the weapon had also grown, its blade large enough to hack Tom in two, the edge gleaming wickedly.

Koba let out a triumphant roar and swung the axe towards Tom's head.

CHAPTER EIGHT

AN OLD ENEMY

Tom sprang aside, rolling across the floor as the axe head came down with a crash into the marble. He bounced to his feet, ready for Koba's next attack.

But it never came. Laughing madly, Koba glided to where Tanner lay sprawled on the floor, his legs kicking as he tried to untangle the chain from around his ankles. But Elenna held the other end, dragging it tight so that Tanner couldn't get free.

She did not see the Beast's approach, nor could she see him raise his deadly axe.

"Look out!" cried Tom, leaping forward to intercept it. The axe glanced off his shield and smashed onto the floor a fraction away from Tanner's head.

"This isn't your fight," Tanner shouted at Tom.

"It is now," Tom replied.

Tanner twisted onto his front, grabbing the chain in both hands and yanking it so that Elenna was pulled off her feet. Silver ran to his mistress's side.

Tom thrust his sword at the Beast's chest and throat, driving him back away from Tanner. Koba, retreating, shape-shifted again – he now wore the form of Tom's Uncle Henry, the kindly blacksmith who had raised him.

"Go home, Tom," said his uncle. "You're not needed any more."

"I don't care who you become!" shouted Tom, advancing, his shield blocking the axe-blows and his sword darting in, seeking a target.

Suddenly, he was facing King Hugo. "Your part in the Quest is over, Tom," said the King. "Let Tanner do the rest."

Setting his jaw, Tom fought on, his sword a silver whirl as he thrust and jabbed. He sensed that the Beast was weakening, as his parries lost power.

"Give up, Koba," Tom shouted, fighting on. "Admit defeat and this will all be over."

The Beast changed shape again, and now Tom was confronted by Captain Harkman, clad in his golden breastplate and scarlet cloak. The Captain brought his axe down hard, but Tom jumped up to avoid it, driving a high kick into his opponent's chest. The Captain skidded across the smooth floor and came to a halt against the wall.

Tom advanced on him, pointing his sword at his throat. "Yield!" he cried.

The Captain's body writhed and re-formed into the pale, slender figure of Aduro's dead apprentice, Marc. He looked pleadingly up at Tom, his chest heaving as he panted for breath. "Remember how I died in Tavania?" he groaned. "It was a blessed relief. I'm happy to die again. Kill me now, Tom."

"I don't want to kill you," Tom said. "Koba – listen to me. Stop fighting and

admit you're defeated."

Marc's face twisted into an ugly smile. "Never," he said. "You will have to kill me to end this."

Even as Marc was speaking, Tom heard Koba's sneer in his head.

"But you don't have it in you to kill me..."

Tom shuddered as he stared into

Marc's eyes. Koba was right – Tom couldn't imagine himself striking a mortal blow at a defenceless Beast.

What happens if Koba never yields?

"Out of my way!" Tom was pushed roughly aside from behind.

Tanner stood over the frail Wizard's apprentice, his sword gripped in both hands. "Now you will die!" he shouted.

Tom barged into Tanner, deflecting the blow so that the blade dug deep into the wall, spraying shards of marble.

"Curse you!" howled Tanner, struggling to free his wedged sword.

Marc crawled away, changing back into Koba's true, dreadful form. The Beast swung a mighty arm, sweeping Tanner off his feet and sending him tumbling across the hall.

Koba pursued, the point of his whirlwind of cloud cracking the marble floor beneath him as he went.

Tanner lay on his back, his chest rising and falling rapidly. Tom ran after Koba as the Beast loomed above the fallen warrior, lifting a clawed hand and preparing to deliver the deadly blow.

"No!" Tom flung himself at Koba, slicing his sword through the Beast's forked claws. Koba let out a bellow of pain and anger as thick amber blood spurted from his wounded fingertips.

The Beast flailed, and struck Tom across the forehead. Stunned by the blow and almost blinded by agony, Tom dropped his sword and fell to his knees.

As he groped helplessly for his fallen blade, he could hear the Beast grunt and snort in fury.

Through flashes of pain, Tom looked up and saw the whirlwind tail whipping towards him. He dived aside as the tail tore a hole in the marble floor, creating a blizzard of stone-chips.

Rolling and squirming across the ground to avoid strike after strike of Koba's tail, Tom found himself trapped in a corner, his back to the wall. The Beast towered above him. The hideous mouth stretched wide again, the orange and green eyes aflame, as Koba rose until the point of the whirlwind was poised above Tom's head.

There was no escape.

Tom raised his shield, expecting a powerful blow.

"It's good to see you again," said a horribly familiar voice. Tom dropped his shield and found himself staring into the face of his old enemy, Malvel. To his horror, he saw that the Evil Wizard had picked up his own sword.

"But..." Tom began. "You're dead."

Malvel lifted the blade. "And soon you'll join me," he said. "You have no idea how much I have longed for this moment!"

Malvel's face twisted into a cruel smile and he thrust the sword at Tom's chest.

CHAPTER NINE

EYE OF FIRE, EYE OF JADE

Malvel stiffened, his sword arm frozen. A grimace of shock and pain contorted his face.

Tom heard Elenna's voice. "The moment you long for will never come!" Malvel tottered forward and fell onto his hands and knees, the sword chiming on the marble as it fell from his fingers. Elenna was standing

behind him, her face grim and pale.

Tom saw that Koba's severed claws jutted from Malvel's back, amber blood oozing down his cloak. Elenna had used the Beast's own weapon against him!

Malvel looked into Tom's eyes, and his face was a white mask of pain. "Does the girl fight your battles for you now?" murmured the Evil Wizard.

Tom stooped over Malvel, almost too exhausted to stand.

He heard Tanner give a moan. The warrior was still lying on the ground with Silver standing guard over him.

Elenna picked up Tom's fallen sword. "We should end this now," she murmured, lifting the sword as if to drive it into Malvel's back alongside the claws. Malvel raised his arms weakly, and before Tom had time to speak, the crouching shape began to change again. It became a slender woman with a delicate face framed by long, lustrous black hair. Kindly eyes gazed up at Elenna from between the cowering woman's fingers.

I've never seen this woman before,

thought Tom. *But...she seems familiar.*

"Mother...?" Elenna gasped, tears sparkling in her eyes.

"My darling daughter," murmured the woman.

Elenna never knew her mother.

Becoming the image of Elenna's lost mother was the cruellest trick that Koba had played. Tom could see the raw pain in Elenna's face. She lowered the sword as the woman got to her feet and staggered backwards.

"My sweet daughter," she said. "Please, don't hurt me again."

Tom strode towards Elenna and wrested his sword from her limp fingers. "That is not your mother," he said firmly. "She died in a fire a long time ago. You *know* that!"

"Yes..." murmured Elenna, gazing at the woman's smiling face. "But..."

Tom turned to the Beast, seething with anger. "I have had enough of your deceptions!" he shouted, pointing the sword at the woman. "You may have twisted Tanner's mind, but you won't do that to me. While there's blood in my veins, I will always fight on the side of Good."

Koba grew back into his true form, but slowly. He pulled himself across the floor with just his arms. Tom saw blobs and streaks of amber blood staining the marble from the wounds to his hand and back.

Tom advanced, sword levelled at Koba's throat. The Beast eyed him, his jaw clenching and his mouth twisted.

"It's over," Tom said quietly.

The great leathery shoulders slumped and the Beast's head

drooped with a long sigh. The fire in Koba's orange eye burned out, and the green eye seemed to glaze over as the Beast began to shrink. As he became smaller, his shape changed again and again, revealing face after face. Men's faces, women's faces, the faces of children and of creatures Tom did not recognise. Sad, miserable, defeated faces.

It's every shape he has ever shifted into!

As he dwindled away, Koba became more and more pale and wraith-like, until he was just a floating shadow. Then there was a swirl of air and even the shadow was gone.

Tom saw something drop. He heard a clinking sound as something green rolled across the floor towards him.

He reached down and picked up the gleaming orb of jade.

This is all that's left of Koba – his green eye.

Tom put the jade orb in his tunic and turned to face Elenna.

"The last Beast is defeated," he said. "Our Quest along the Warrior's Road is finished."

But even as he spoke, the whole hall filled with a rumbling and a grinding noise. The floor shook under his feet and the walls and ceiling began to topple.

Elenna and Silver rushed to Tom's side as the marble began to crash down, throwing up clouds of dust and sending splinters of stone flying through the air.

Tom saw the red glow of the Warrior's Road beyond the doorway.

"That way!" he shouted. "Let's go!"

He looked around for Tanner, and through the raining debris he saw the first Master of the Beasts. He was standing tall and straight, his body clad in the shining Golden Armour, his long dark hair framing his noble face. All trace of Koba's evil corruption was gone.

"Come with us," Tom called, running desperately for the doorway with Elenna and Silver.

"My Quests are done," called Tanner, his body wreathed in smoke and dust as the hall fell to pieces all around him. "I will rest in peace now."

"No!" Tom hesitated in the doorway.

"Quickly, Tom, or you'll be killed!" Elenna caught hold of his arm and dragged him through the doorway a moment before its arch collapsed.

The last thing Tom saw was Tanner raising a hand in farewell as he was engulfed in the tumbling marble.

Then a wind snatched at Tom, sucking him into darkness.

The shrieking gale died away and Tom felt solid ground under his feet.

He looked around, gasping for breath and waiting to feel the elation of victory. But, for some reason, he didn't…

"It's the courtyard of King Hugo's palace!" Elenna cried. "Tom – we've been brought back safely!"

Tom eyed his companions. "Apparently so," he said. Silver was bounding around Elenna's legs, overjoyed to be home again.

Tom felt a strange urge to smack the wolf on the muzzle with the flat of his blade. He wasn't sure why he was so angry, but he liked the feeling.

"We should go to the throne room," said Elenna. "King Hugo will want to hear the good news."

Tom followed Elenna and Silver into the palace and through rooms and halls until they came at last to the throne room. A cloaked and hooded figure sat on the high throne.

Elenna started forward. "Your Majesty—"

The figure lifted its head and the hood fell back to reveal the face of the Judge, Jezrin.

"Greetings," he hissed.

CHAPTER TEN

KING TOM?

Elenna let out a gasp of dismay and Silver snarled.

"Where is King Hugo?" asked Tom, striding up to the dais.

A small, shambling figure in a court jester's costume appeared from behind the throne. The three-pointed hat on his head jingled. "Jezrin has placed him in the dungeons."

Tom recognised the face and the voice,

both full of anguish and humiliation. "Aduro," he said, grinning. "I see our new ruler has been kind enough to give you a job fit for your abilities."

"Tom!" Elenna gasped. "Why would you say such a thing? What's wrong with you?"

Tom looked at her, shrugging. "Let's just say I've seen sense," he said coldly.

"Well done, Tom," said the Judge, standing up and gesturing towards the throne. "Would you care to take a seat, my boy?"

"Yes," Tom said. "I would." He mounted the dais, ignoring the small, horrified voice in his brain telling him: *This is all wrong. Don't do it!*

But how could it be wrong? Surely it was Tom's *destiny* to rule Avantia?

Tanner was right – defeating Koba has filled you with evil. You must fight it.

"Shut up!" Tom shouted, wanting to silence the irritating voice in his head.

He turned and sat on the throne. Elenna stared at him in despair. He smiled at her then looked at Aduro, who was standing there with his mouth hanging open in shock.

"You look more the fool than ever, Aduro," said Tom, settling himself on

the throne. Silver growled, baring his teeth. "Elenna, if you don't shut that mongrel up, I'll have him caged!"

The Judge let out a laugh. "This is even better than I had hoped," he said, resting his hand on Tom's shoulder. "It was never my plan for you to die on the Road, Tom. I wanted you to return – new and improved." His voice rose to a roar. "And now we will rule the kingdom of Avantia together."

Elenna stumbled forward. "Tom, you know this is wrong," she pleaded.

She's telling the truth! Listen to her!

"Be quiet!" shouted Tom, glaring at Elenna.

"You're wasting your breath," Aduro sighed. "Tom is under a powerful spell. He can't help himself."

"Silence, you old fool," snapped Tom. "Guards!" he called. Armed men ran from the shadows. "Throw this girl in the dungeons." He grinned. "In a cell near to our former king, Hugo – let *him* suffer her endless whining."

Two men caught hold of Elenna and began to drag her away.

"This isn't you!" she called to Tom.

"Is it not?" said Tom with a laugh. "Why can't I be King? I think I will make a very good ruler." He narrowed his eyes. "So long as the people do exactly as I tell them."

Silver rushed to his mistress's aid, but the Judge raised a hand. Strands of purple light flowed from his fingers, gathering around the wolf and hardening into a small cage. Silver snarled and leaped at the bars, but fell back yelping as they sizzled and sparked at his touch.

Elenna glared at the Judge. "You

won't get away with this," she shouted, struggling as the two soldiers towed her to the doorway. "While there's blood in my veins, I'll never stop fighting to save Tom from you!"

Tom leaned forward on the throne, staring hard at her.

While there's blood in my veins…

A dark fog seemed to lift from his mind for a moment.

Those are your *words. You know they are!*

Puzzled, Tom slid his hand into his tunic, feeling something small and hard and cold under his fingers. He pulled it out and looked down at the green orb that lay in his palm.

"Koba's eye," he muttered slowly under his breath.

Aduro's voice drifted into his head. *"…a powerful spell. He can't help himself."*

Tom closed his fist around the orb, sensing its strength, enjoying the way it made him feel.

"That's it," said the Judge. "Embrace the power, Tom. It belongs to you."

But confusion raged in Tom's mind.

I want this power...but it isn't right. I want to rule...but the throne belongs to King Hugo – not to me.

"Give me the Orb of Jade," said the Judge. "I will look after it for you."

Tom looked up at the Wizard. There was greed in the man's eyes. Greed and malice.

He held out his hand, ready to drop the orb into the Judge's open palm.

No!

"I can't..." he murmured, jerking his hand back and dropping the orb. It rolled away and clinked as it struck the stone dais. He looked at it for a moment, then raised his foot.

Destroy it. Release yourself...

"No! You can't!" screamed the Judge. "Not when I am this close to victory!"

Tom brought his heel down hard on the orb. The green ball exploded into dust. Rays of emerald light shot out in all directions. One beam struck the Judge between the eyes. Another hit the cage containing Silver, dissolving it to dust. Jezrin writhed, howling, as he

was consumed by green fire.

Tom clenched his eyes tightly as all the darkness and confusion was swept from his mind. When he opened his eyes again, the Judge had vanished too. Silver rushed at the soldiers holding his mistress. They cowered back, and Elenna broke free, running towards the throne, her face alight with hope.

"Are you all right, Tom?" she asked.

Blood rushed to Tom's face as shame overwhelmed him. "It was Koba's eye that made the victor evil," he murmured. "I almost succumbed. If it hadn't been for you..."

Elenna grinned. "That doesn't matter now," she said.

Aduro tore off his jester's cap and turned to the soldiers. "The rule of Jezrin is over," he called. "Go to the dungeons and release Avantia's true King – and my former apprentice."

The soldiers gave the old Wizard a quick bow then ran for the doors.

"Where *is* Jezrin?" Tom asked.

"I cannot say for sure," Aduro replied. "Banished to a place far away, I hope. With any luck, he may never return."

He turned to Tom, resting a hand on his shoulder. "You walked the Warrior's Road as a hero," Aduro said. "You can now truly call yourself Master of the Beasts." He smiled. "Not that I ever doubted that you were worthy of the title."

Tom's heart filled with joy, but it was tempered with sadness when he recalled the fallen heroes in the chamber of coffins. "Every Master of the Beasts was a hero," he said, "whether he walked the Road to its end or died on the Quest."

King Hugo strode in, his beard shaggy and unkempt, his robes filthy. Behind him, Daltec was using his magic to light the candles in the chamber. Soon it was bathed in brilliant white light.

King Hugo smiled when his eyes fell on Tom and Elenna. "I knew you wouldn't fail your kingdom," he said.

Tom gestured towards the throne. "Take a seat, Your Majesty. The Judge is gone and Avantia is safe again. And while there's blood in my veins, I vow that I will fight any Evil that threatens our realm!" He turned to the gathered guards, who joined him in his chant as he raised his sword: "Long live King Hugo! And long live the Kingdom of Avantia!"

Join Tom on the next stage
of the Beast Quest!

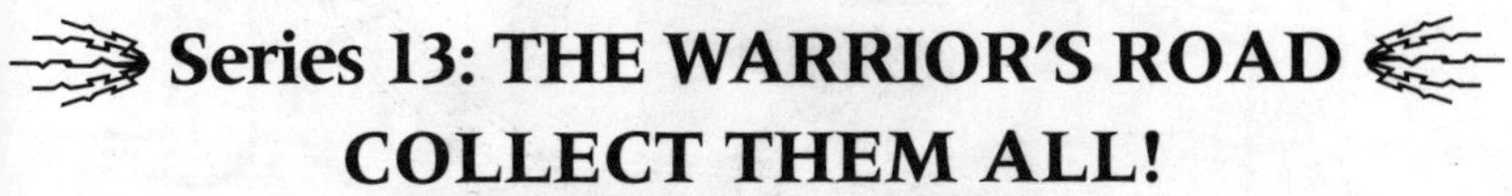

Series 13: THE WARRIOR'S ROAD COLLECT THEM ALL!

The Warrior's Road is Tom's toughest challenge yet. Will he succeed where so many have failed?

978 1 40832 402 8

978 1 40832 403 5

978 1 40832 404 2

978 1 40832 405 9

978 1 40832 406 6

978 1 40832 407 3

 Series 14: THE CURSED DRAGON

Coming soon!

Meet four terrifying new Beasts!

Raffkor the Stampeding Brute
Vislak the Slithering Serpent
Tikron the Jungle Master
Falra the Snow Phoenix

Watch out for the next Special Bumper Edition OUT OCTOBER 2013!

Win an exclusive
Beast Quest T-shirt and goody bag!

In every Beast Quest book the Beast Quest logo is hidden in one of the pictures. Find the logos in books 73 to 78 and make a note of which pages they appear on. Write the six page numbers on a postcard and send it in to us.

Each month we will draw one winner to receive a Beast Quest T-shirt and goody bag.

THE BEAST QUEST COMPETITION:
The Warrior's Road
Orchard Books
338 Euston Road, London NW1 3BH
Australian readers should email:
childrens.books@hachette.com.au

New Zealand readers should write to:
Beast Quest Competition
4 Whetu Place, Mairangi Bay, Auckland, NZ
or email: childrensbooks@hachette.co.nz

Only one entry per child.
Final draw: January 2014

You can also enter this competition via the Beast Quest website: www.beastquest.co.uk

Join the Quest,
Join the Tribe

www.beastquest.co.uk

Have you checked out the Beast Quest website? It's the place to go for games, downloads, activities, sneak previews and lots of fun!

You can read all about your favourite Beasts, download free screensavers and desktop wallpapers for your computer, and even challenge your friends to a Beast Tournament.

Sign up to the newsletter at www.beastquest.co.uk to receive exclusive extra content and the opportunity to enter special members-only competitions. We'll send you up-to-date info on all the Beast Quest books, including the next exciting series which features four brand-new Beasts!

Get 30% off all Beast Quest Books at www.beastquest.co.uk
Enter the code BEAST at the checkout.

Offer valid in UK and ROI, offer expires December 2013

LOOK OUT FOR SERIES 2:

THE CAVERN OF GHOSTS

OUT SEPTEMBER 2013

978 1 40832 411 0

978 1 40832 412 7

978 1 40832 413 4

978 1 40832 414 1

978 1 40831 852 2

COMING SOON!

SPECIAL BUMPER EDITION

www.seaquestbooks.co.uk